Kids love reading
Choose Your Own Adventure®!

"These books are like games. Sometimes the choice seems like it will solve everything, but you wonder if it's a trap."

Matt Harmon, age 11

"I think you'd call this a book for active readers, and I am definitely an active reader!"

Ava Kendrick, age 11

"You decide your own fate, but your fate is still a surprise."

Chun Tao Lin, age 10

"Come on in this book if you're crazy enough! One wrong move and you're a goner!"

Ben Curley, age 9

"You can read Choose Your Own Adventure books so many wonderful ways. You could go find your dog or follow a unicorn."

Celia Lawton, 11

**Ask your bookseller for books you have missed
or visit us at cyoa.com to collect them all.**

CHOOSE YOUR OWN ADVENTURE® 35

BEHIND THE WHEEL

BY R. A. MONTGOMERY

COVER ART BY WES LOUIE
INTERIOR ILLUSTRATED BY SITTISAN SUNDARAVEJ

CHOOSECO
WAITSFIELD, VERMONT

Cover art: Wes Louie
Interior art: Sittisan Sundaravej
Book design: Stacey Boyd, Big Eyedea Visual Design

For information regarding permission, write to:

CHOOSECO
P.O. Box 46
Waitsfield, Vermont 05673
www.cyoa.com

ISBN 1-933390-35-2
EAN 978-1-933390-35-2

Published simultaneously in the United States and Canada

Printed in the United States

0 9 8 7 6 5 4 3 2 1

BEWARE and WARNING!

This book is different from other books.

You and YOU ALONE are in charge of what happens in this story.

There are dangers, choices, adventures, and consequences. YOU must use all of your numerous talents and much of your enormous intelligence. The wrong decision could end in disaster—even death. But, don't despair. At any time, YOU can go back and make another choice, alter the path of your story, and change its result.

You've always dreamed of racing cars. Finally your chance has arrived! Your cousin has lent you his race car and you are ready to race a rally that runs through Germany, France, and Switzerland. Not everyone in the race plays fair—there are offers of bribes, and even sabotage! Your car alone is not going to win. Be on your toes because the race is on!

You can't believe it—it's your big day and it's raining! Drops pound the asphalt, turning fuel spills into watery puddles. Lights from the huge towers surrounding the roadway glitter on the surface as rainbow colors rise from the pavement.

The officials have delayed the race until the storm passes. Disappointed, you slowly start over to where you parked your car. As you approach it, you're startled by a familiar-looking figure bent over the engine, fiddling with a wrench.

"Hey! Stop that! What are you doing to my car?" you shout.

"I'm fixing it for you," the figure says, standing upright. When you see the face, your heart lurches in your chest. It's scraped and bloody, muscles and tendons fully exposed. "You crashed."

"What do you mean?" you scream at this grotesque figure.

"Just that. We crashed. Don't you remember? I'm you and you're me. Just look at yourself."

You wake with a start, not quite sure of where you are. Then you remember. You're in Geneva, Switzerland at your cousin Hubert's house. He is a motor-racing fanatic, and you share his love of race cars. For the last three summers you've spent your vacations with him, learning all there is to know about racing. But this is the summer the two of you have been waiting for.

Turn to page 2.

2

This summer there will be re-creations of two famous European races: the Alpine Rally and the premier Grand Prix event called the Nürburgring. To your astonishment, Hubert wants you to drive one of his prized vintage cars in the race of your choice. You're sure that this is the cause of your nightmare; you're excited but you're nervous, too.

Your cousin Hubert is fifteen years older than you are. He's not a professional racer; he is a banker. But race cars are his pride and joy. He owns only machines of the fifties and sixties and often he says, "They don't make them that way anymore." You tend to agree—they were the cars with precision, personality, and style.

Hubert loves the smell of fuel and oil, and he thrives on the danger that permeates the world of high-performance cars. He idolizes drivers of the past such as Nuvolari, Fangio, Count de Portago, and Stirling Moss. Today, however, Hubert says that racing has become a big business. For him it has lost some of its glory, and this summer's races will surely fill him with nostalgia.

Turn to page 4.

"It's the Ferrari and the Grand Prix for me," you finally say. "So what now?" you add, unsure of what you need to do in this dream-come-true sequence of events.

"Well, my friend, we need to get the car ready, trailer it up to Germany, and check the course."

"How much practice will I get?" you ask with a hint of concern in your voice. The Nürburgring, as you know, is one of the toughest races in the world.

"The whole week before the race. They don't want accidents any more than we do. But remember, practice is practice. The race will be different."

"Do I practice in the Ferrari?" you ask.

"No. We will practice in an ordinary car," Hubert answers.

"An ordinary car, Hubert? Hey, what kind of practice is that?" Your pre-race jitters are getting worse.

"Familiarity with the course is the key to success, or I should say, one of the keys."

Turn to page 18.

4

The Grand Prix race at the German Nürburgring course has a 14.3 mile lap. It is torturous,
with 85 major turns to the right, and 89 to the left,
totaling 3,828 corners in the twenty-two-lap race.
The course goes through forests and mountain
passes, along steep ravines, and around a tough
hairpin. It is always demanding. The Eifel
Mountains, near the Belgian border, play host to
this speed race. Getting across the finish line first is
what counts.

For this race Hubert has a rebuilt 1954 red Ferrari supercharged 2 liter. The car earned its stripes for two seasons on the Grand Prix circuit before spinning out of control, crashing a barrier, and flipping three times at Monte Carlo in 1963. It was withdrawn from racing and eventually sold off as a curiosity. Hubert keeps it beautiful and ready to eat up the road and his competitors.

Turn to page 7.

6

"The Alpine Rally sounds fabulous, Hubert. I think I'll try that race."

"Perfect, my cousin. If the truth be known, that is my real preference. In many ways the Alpine Rally is the king of motor sports. Bravo, then. I'll join you in the rally."

You feel the slightest bit of regret about leaving the big red Ferrari in the barn. But choices are what life is all about, you think, turning your attention to the silver Porsche.

"What about the navigator? Will you be my navigator, Hubert?"

"No, as I said before, the daughter of my friend Albert Dumont will be your navigator. Marie-Lise has been living in Argentina for the last six years. I don't think you have ever met her, but you will like her, I assure you. And this will not be her first rally. She has become quite proficient navigating for her father in club races over the last three years."

"Great! When do I meet her?"

"This afternoon. Let's get packed, First we'll need to take a look at the course. We'll take two cars. Come, let's get moving."

"I'm on my way," you say, taking the stairs two at a time to get to your bedroom and pack. It doesn't take long. Everything you need fits into a large backpack. Hubert packs two leather suitcases.

Turn to page 22.

You know that Grand Prix racing depends on cornering (getting your car through a turn in the most efficient way possible), the ability of the driver, and the design of the machine. If tires, brakes, gears, engine, or nerves fail, the race is lost.

The other race is a re-creation of the two thousand mile Alpine Rally. The cars must climb over massive mountain passes on little more than goat trails with no guardrails and then zoom along the Monza racetrack. It is the king of all the rallies—difficult, exhausting, and dangerous.

Rallying is very different from Grand Prix racing. The rally is not a speed race; it is a test of car and driver over a given route. What matters in a rally is average speed. To measure this, a committee decides in advance exactly how much time at a designated speed is needed to cover a given section of the course. Spread out over five days, the Alpine Rally includes hill climbs, acceleration tests, braking, and stops and starts. The rally is a true measure of a machine's reliability.

Turn to the next page.

8

Instead of cars designed only for racing, as in the case of the Grand Prix, rally cars are standard models, but they are modified. Also, in a rally, inside the car is a team of two—a driver and a navigator. The navigator carries a clipboard marking the time, distances, and locations of the sections of the circuit and the checkpoints. Timekeeping, hazard spotting, and co-driving are the primary responsibilities of the navigator. These rallies are long, grueling affairs that require stamina and nerve—that is why it is a team effort.

For the Alpine Rally, Hubert has a small silver Porsche Carrera. It was built in 1962 and lovingly maintained by Hubert from the day he picked it up at the factory in Stuttgart, Germany. Dents have never marred the fine aluminum body, and the leather interior, although cracked by sun in a few places, still has a lustrous black gleam. However, this is no usual, run-of-the-mill Porsche. Hubert has had this car modified so that it can compete with almost anything the rally can throw at it. The suspension, wheels, brakes, carburetion, and engine have all undergone a subtle transformation.

Turn to the next page.

10

You must make a choice between these two magnificent races. You told your cousin Hubert that you would make your decision this morning, by breakfast. Pushing all traces of your horrible nightmare aside, you rise from your bed, get dressed, and greet your cousin on his terrace.

"Well, good morning," Hubert says to you in his lightly accented English. "The time has come. Have you made your decision? I can see you helmeted and goggled, roaring down the stretches at Nürburgring, going high into the corners, accelerating toward the finish line!"

You like the image. He continues.

"I could just as well see you skirting the thousand-foot ravines in the rally, surefooted as any mountain goat. And racing along with you will be Marie-Lise, my Swiss navigator. I will be so proud when you and my Porsche win!"

It's unbelievable still that you can be the driver in either one of these events. But you've trained, and you're ready—you know it. It's a tough choice, but you must make up your mind now, just as you promised Hubert you would.

However, before you make your choice, you should know that something very important is going on right now in a café in Paris. Through the power of thought travel, you have the ability to take this journey and listen in on a private conversation that could affect your life . . . or death.

Go on to the next page.

It's late afternoon in Paris. A small café sits on an unremarkable street filled with old apartment houses. The café is called the Trois Copains or "The Three Buddies," and at this time of day it seems unusually empty.

A large black sedan pulls up to the café and stops. Three people get out. There's an older man, perhaps in his sixties, white-haired, mustached, and elegant. He is escorted by a tall, auburn-haired woman in her early twenties. She in turn is followed by another man, also in his early twenties. He is dark, short, and broad-shouldered. He scans the area before they all enter the café.

You observe all of this from above, through the power of thought travel. Though you are keenly aware of what is happening, your thought journey has a foggy, dreamlike quality to it.

Turn to page 13.

Moments later you see a man on a moped arrive at the café. He is less well dressed than the others, looking more like a worker. As he walks into the cafe, you notice that the heel of one of his shoes is several inches thicker than the other.

"What would you say if I told you that these people were planning your death?" a voice inside your head asks. "That's right, your death. Right here in this little out-of-the-way café, your fate is about to be decided. Come, let's listen in."

At first you are jarred by this voice, its tone strange and yet familiar. Then you realize that it is your thought guide, and you give in to it, allowing yourself to go along for the ride.

Turn to the next page.

14

"The driver is young?" the older man says. "Young, but good, or so they say," the woman comments.

"Courage?" the short man asks.

"Most definitely," the old man answers. "Smart, too."

The short man speaks again. "So you think this one is a winner, then?"

"We'll fix that. Don't worry for even a moment," the worker says, laughing.

The short man shakes his head. "You talk big, but—"

"The family is American and filthy rich," the older man interrupts.

"Ah, the picture becomes clearer."

A waiter scurries in with a tray of glasses and two bottles of water. The group stops talking upon his arrival. They seem impatient, waiting for him to leave.

Everyone looks up as a man in an expensive pin-striped suit joins the group. He is fit, suntanned, perhaps in his late thirties. He wears dark glasses, which he doesn't bother to remove in the gloom of the café.

Turn to the next page.

16

"Late as usual, Raoul," the white-haired man says.

"Your sense of time is of little or no importance to me, Eric," Raoul says. "You should know that by now." He draws up a chair and sits comfortably in it.

"Someday it will catch up with you, you know. It always does," Eric continues.

Raoul laughs. "Threats, Eric, always threats. Don't you get bored with yourself? Let's stop wasting time and get to the subject at hand— money. What's the plan?"

"This young American driver is the key to our winning. This will be a great coup! People put a great deal of money on these races. But only we will know in advance who wins." Eric looks at all the people at the table with great intensity. He folds his hands and nods at the man with the large heel. "Or perhaps a simple kidnapping will change the odds."

"There will be no problem with most of the cars. I have a mechanic's pass for the Grand Prix and the Alpine Rally," the worker says, massaging his ankle.

Go on to the next page.

"What will you do?" Raoul asks.

"Brakes will fail, carburetors will clog, tires will either come off rims or blow apart. I have my ways," the worker answers.

"I am sure of that, Henri. We all know of your work. I hope you will be careful that you are not recognized," Eric comments.

"Have no fear. Look." Henri opens a valise and displays a professional actor's makeup kit.

"Again, about the American? How do we deal with this racer?" Eric asks.

"Leave that to me," Raoul replies. "We will find a way. If the American won't play, then the American will become, as they say, history. I myself prefer blackmail, however."

You can't believe what you're hearing—these people are talking about you!

"Come, we must return," the voice guides you. "Hubert is still waiting for your decision."

Before you realize what has happened, you are back on the terrace with your cousin Hubert. It's as if no time has passed. You are about to choose the event you wish to race in, now forewarned about the possibility of foul play.

If you decide to drive the Ferrari in the Grand Prix, turn to page 3.

If you decide to drive the Porsche in the Alpine Rally, turn to page 6.

That afternoon, you and Hubert load the Ferrari onto a trailer, hitch it to a brand-new Range Rover, and head off for Germany on the autoroute out of Geneva. Excitement rushes through you. You can't believe Hubert has placed so much trust and confidence in you, and you're glad he's staying with you for the race.

The afternoon drifts by. Daydreams of racing victory delight you, and you push aside that disturbing nightmare you had where you saw yourself the victim of a horrific fatal crash. After all, crashes are a part of auto racing. You try to be aware of this but not morbid, keeping yourself humble, and your wits about you.

Turn to the next page.

20

You finally reach the famous Nürburgring race course in Germany. It's laid out in gorgeous surroundings. And today with no one on the track it's quiet.

After you look over the course, you take rooms in a small old hotel in the town of Quiddelbach, within fourteen miles of the Nürburgring circuit.

"Aren't you Hubert D'Albert?" a suntanned, well-dressed man says, rising when the two of you enter the hotel lobby.

"Why, yes I am," your cousin replies. "And you, sir?"

"Raoul Desjardin, at your service. I have been impressed with your career in both banking and sport motoring," he continues. You notice that he is in his late thirties, in good shape, and handsome. "I'm here with my mechanic. Unfortunately, my car is beyond repair for the race. So, allow me to offer you our services—without pay, of course. It would be my great pleasure."

Raoul turns to you and smiles in a reassuring way. You have a faint recollection of seeing this man someplace before. You aren't sure where or when—it is all very foggy and vague.

Turn to page 28.

"Excuse me, but I just remembered that I'm supposed to pick up the extra tires this afternoon, the ones with the special treads," you say. It is only a half lie—you are supposed to pick them up, but not until tomorrow.

"Can't it wait?" Marie-Lise asks, a look of surprise on her face.

"No, I'm sorry. I hate to leave a thing undone. Just tell my cousin Hubert that I'll be back after dinner. See you," you say as you head out the door.

Moments later you are driving out of the village walls and down the winding road into the valley. You have no idea where you are going, but you need the time to think and settle your fears.

"What do I do now?" you say out loud.

As if in response, something inside you tells you to follow your instinct. You're doing well so far. But don't run too far. You don't want them to get suspicious.

Turn to page 27.

"We'll pick up Marie-Lise at her house. It's a stone building in the Veille Ville or Old Town section of Geneva," Hubert says.

Hubert drives his Range Rover, and you handle the Porsche. It's like a well-trained jungle cat, lithe and quick and powerful.

When you arrive at Marie-Lise's house, you quickly bond as the two of you have a lot in common.

Marie-Lise introduces you to her uncle, a white-haired man in his sixties who looks amazingly like the man you saw in the café in Paris. You try to convince yourself that the whole strange Paris experience was a daydream, but the fear of the man and his companions remains.

Later that afternoon, Marie-Lise sits next to you in the Porsche as the car turns out of Switzerland and into France. Hubert plans to join the two of you at a hotel along the way.

After four hours of driving, you turn off the auto-route and head for a small village called Venasque.

Turn to the next page.

"We're supposed to stay in a place called L'Auberge de la Fontaine. It's in the center of the village," you comment as the Porsche winds its way up the hillside to the walled medieval town. There is a somber and brooding sense to the village.

"Here it is," Marie-Lise says. L'Auberge de la Fontaine is in a beautiful old stone building facing the small town square with its ornate fountain. It is charming, but when you enter the dark foyer of the hotel, you are gripped with fear. There, checking in at the small desk, is the man called Raoul from the café in Paris.

"Raoul, what a surprise," Marie-Lise exclaims, but there is no warmth in her greeting. Raoul turns and greets the two of you with a smile.

"Your Uncle Eric said you would be staying here, Marie-Lise, so I chose to join you two. I hope that I will not be a burden."

"Never, Raoul, never. How could you ever be a burden to anyone?" Marie-Lise says, almost sarcastically. Raoul extends his hand to you in greeting.

Turn to the next page.

26

You want to get out of the hotel as fast as you can. This man, despite his apparent charm and warmth, frightens you. Your instinct says to leave immediately, but being polite, you do not move just yet.

If you decide to leave immediately,
turn to page 21.

If you continue to be polite and stay for now,
turn to page 30.

Your thoughts linger in your mind as you decide what to do. Realizing your inner voice is right and you probably shouldn't arouse their suspicions, you hastily turn around in the narrow street and head back for Venasque.

Parking in front of the hotel, you wait for your cousin Hubert to arrive. You have made up your mind—you're going to tell Hubert about what you overheard in the café in Paris, and you'll try to convince him to drop out of the race.

Hours slip by, and by midnight there has been no sign of Hubert.

"I quit! I want out of this rally, out of this car, and out of this country! I want to go home!" you shout in frustration. Then you slam the car in gear and roar off for the closest airport and a flight back home. You feel bad about just leaving Hubert behind, but you hope he'll understand when you call with your explanation.

The End

"Thank you for your splendid offer, Raoul," Hubert says. He turns to you. "We could use the help. What do you think? Should we let them join our team?"

You feel uneasy about letting complete strangers join the team, and Raoul gives you the creeps. But you do need all the help you can get. Maybe your fears are just more pre-race jitters.

If you agree to let Raoul help you out, turn to page 34.

If you decide to stall for time and get to know Raoul and his mechanic better, turn to page 43.

30

You rein in your panic and remain cordial. Part of you thinks your fear of Raoul is pre-race jitters, a common phenomenon for all competitors. Whatever is going on, your intuition says to remain cautious.

Your room is on the fourth floor of the stone building. It is in stark contrast to the village, for when the door is opened, you suddenly enter a world of modern design. Stainless steel and leather chairs, white walls, and two abstract paintings line the interior. The effect is jarring, and for a moment, you wonder if this is another dream. Walking tentatively into this room, you reach out and touch the steel and leather chair to be sure that it is real. It is.

"Dinner at seven-thirty," Raoul says cheerfully as he stops by your room. "Your cousin should be here by then. I think you'll find the food extraordinarily good here."

"Great. See you then," you reply.

Moments later, you slip out of the room and tiptoe down the stairs, not quite sure why you are being so careful. Your instincts lead you to the parking area outside the hotel. There are some thirty cars there.

"I wonder which one is Raoul's," you ask yourself out loud.

"What was that?" a voice asks.

Go on to the next page.

A man steps out from the shadows. He is short, stocky, bearded, and wearing blue overalls.

"Oh, nothing. Just talking to myself," you say. There is something vaguely familiar about this man, and your instincts now tell you to leave the car park immediately.

You walk briskly but return forty minutes later. After you scout the area, you begin a survey of the cars. Your Porsche is on the outer rim of cars. There are lots of Peugeots, Renaults, BMWs, and a few Volvos. Then you see it.

Huddled up to the wall is a dark green Maserati with Monte Carlo plates. You are sure that this is Raoul's, since Marie-Lise has told you where Raoul is from. Approaching cautiously, you examine the car from the wheels up, your eyes finally coming to rest on the interior. In the evening light, you can make out a cellular phone, a duffel bag filled to capacity, and on the backseat a briefcase.

Turn to the next page.

"Can I help you?" comes a voice, sounding anything but helpful.

"Oh, no. No, nothing. Just looking. It's a beautiful car. Just looking," you stammer. It is the man in the blue overalls. You still can't place him, and you're upset that he's been watching you.

"Well, look all you like, but don't touch."

"No problem," you say as you walk off. "Good night."

Later that night, under cover of darkness, you return to the car park. The briefcase was the same one, you think, that the white-haired man had on the table in the café in Paris. You must find out what's inside. You try the door and find that it is locked. But when you examine the car more closely, you find that the window on the passenger side is open a crack.

You hesitate while your conscience kicks in. It's a crime to do what you are considering doing. But you are sure that Raoul is up to no good. He may even be plotting your death!

You have to do something, but what?

Go on to the next page.

Your first thought is to keep an eye on the car during the night. But that would mean losing sleep, and you decide to think of a more practical plan.

Perhaps you should just go ahead and take the briefcase.

Then again, perhaps you should leave the briefcase alone and keep a cautious eye on Raoul.

If you decide to take the briefcase, turn to page 40.

If you decide to leave the briefcase and exercise caution, turn to page 46.

34

Raoul stands patiently, confidently awaiting your reply. Despite the nagging feeling that there is something troublesome about him, you nod in silent agreement.

"Well, good. Then that's settled," Raoul says, slapping you gently on the shoulders. "Let's get to it. My mechanic, a fine fellow from Marseilles, will join us. Come, let's take a close look at your beauty."

"Great idea," Hubert says. "Follow us."

Go on to the next page.

You lead the way to the trailer and the canvas-shrouded Ferrari. Standing next to the trailer is a man in blue overalls. He is short, with a dark complexion and heavily muscled shoulders. From his lips dangles a wooden toothpick. He removes it, flings it to the ground, and crushes it under his boot. You notice that the heel of his left boot is higher than that of the right.

"Oh, this is my mechanic, Henri," Raoul finally says.

Henri nods but does not speak. Without asking or being told, Henri removes the canvas and reveals the Ferrari as if he were unveiling a famous painting. The car shines in the bright sunlight, and a surge of pride and excitement flows through you. You can't believe you will be driving this car. For a shadow of a moment you feel guilty and unworthy of the honor.

Turn to the next page.

"This is a beauty. This car will win. I can feel it in my bones," Henri says as he runs a hand over the hood.

"Well, let's get it down and give it a spin," Hubert says merrily.

"A pleasure," Raoul replies.

Carefully the Ferrari is rolled off the trailer, its tires scrunching on the gravel of the parking area.

"Can we actually drive it to the course from here?" you ask.

"Yes, we can. You will be issued antique car plates, and you are free to drive it." Raoul seems extremely well-informed. "While Henri and your

cousin go through the formalities, why don't you and I take a drive in my car and take a good look at the course?"

Raoul turns to Henri and speaks rapidly to him in a dialect that you don't understand. Henri seems to jump when Raoul gives him orders.

"I've just told my man to arrange for fueling and oil supplies, as well as all the extras that we might need, you know, spark plugs, fuel filters."

"But we have our own," you counter.

"Well, I like to be sure about these things. We'll use the ones I provide."

Turn to the next page.

38

It worries you that this man has taken over command from Hubert so quickly and easily. Hubert gets so engrossed with cars and racing that he sometimes doesn't see what is going on around him.

Go on to the next page.

Raoul however, does seem to be helpful. There is an air of confidence about him that is attractive. At least he is strong and decisive, you think.

"There's my car. You drive," he says, holding out a leather key case. The car is a Chubasco Maserati. It looks sharklike with its narrow hood and dorsal stabilizer. The side vents look like gill slits. It certainly doesn't have the subtle elegance of the older cars, but the ferociousness of the car is quite a lure.

Hubert is busily fussing with his Ferrari. Half of you wants to go with Raoul for a trial spin around the Nürburgring circuit, but your other half speaks of caution and loyalty to Hubert.

*If you refuse and stay with Hubert,
turn to page 51.*

If you accept Raoul's offer, turn to page 77.

40

The temptation is too great, you decide. You've got to know what's inside that briefcase. After all, you reason, you know from overhearing the conversation in Paris that these people are planning to fix the rally for gambling purposes.

Carefully you slip your fingers in the crack of the open window. It yields to your push. Inch by inch the window lowers until you can stick your whole hand inside and lift the door button. You hope that there isn't an alarm system.

"Yikes!" you scream suddenly, jumping back from the car.

A cat scrambles across the seat, then out of the car at high speed. You've never been so scared in your life. You take a few minutes to recover, then continue, reaching for the car's door handle.

Go on to the next page.

Instantly, the door clicks open. You snake your hand inside, grasp the smooth leather handle of

the briefcase, and withdraw it in one swift move. You close the door and start to run away but then realize that you have left the window open.

You ease the door open once again and kick at the ground when you discover that the windows are electric.

There's nothing that you can do, so you close the door again. By morning the break-in will be discovered. Too late now, you decide, as you carefully make your way back inside the hotel.

The stairs do not creak, and soon you are relieved to be back in your room.

After you lock the door, you concentrate on the contents of the briefcase. You're discouraged when you notice a combination lock on the top. You know the odds are against it, but you hope that maybe, just maybe, the right numbers were left in place.

You give it a try, and click! The briefcase opens!

Turn to the next page.

42

There, lying in the case, are several photographs of you. There is also a sheaf of banking documents, mostly financial statements of your family's business. In addition are several pages describing your parents' divorce and their current living arrangements. One paragraph stands out:

Their only child spends summers in Europe because the parents can't agree on who gets the summer visitation rights. This child could be held for a very large ransom.

Your suspicions are correct. These people are worse than gamblers—they're kidnappers!

But before you decide what to do, your door is forced open, the lights then go off, and you hear Raoul's treacherous laughter.

Over your short imprisonment as a hostage, you learn you were worth more to your parents than the awesome sum in euros they paid for your release. You knew when they hugged you at the airport, it was for love. You are very important to both of them.

The End

"Cousin Hubert, let me bring the bags up, then I'll be right back," you say. "What now?" you ask yourself as you run to your room. You sense that this man could be dangerous. You struggle with your memory, trying desperately to jog it.

Images of a hot day and a narrow street in a city flood your brain, but nothing is clear. Snatches of conversation drift into place, distorted just enough to be incomprehensible.

Then, with a flash, you remember.

"The café in Paris! The gamblers! He's one of them! This could mean my death!" As suddenly as the memory comes, it vanishes, leaving only fear as a residue.

"I've got to get out of here and warn the police! I've got to get Hubert away from that guy! I know what I'll do. I'll get in touch with Interpol. They'll help." You are so frightened that you speak out loud.

Within seconds you have run down the steep, narrow old stairway to the main floor. There is a doorway to the right. You open it.

Turn to page 45.

Looking first to the left, then the right, you step out into the bright July sunshine.

"Going somewhere, my young friend?" comes a voice. The speaker is a man with unruly blond hair. It looks like a wig, but you're not sure. Your attention is drawn to his left foot. The heel on the boot is thicker than the one on the other foot.

"Just for a walk," you reply.

"I think you had better come with me," he says, as you notice a small black revolver in his right hand. He does not smile.

Suddenly the fog clears. He is the man on the moped you saw in Paris! But did that even happen? Or was it all a dream? The gun, however, is real enough.

You follow him. You are soon reported as missing. Amazingly, you escape from a basement cell in a 16th century villa in northern Italy outside Milan. The race is over, but you are alive!

The End

46

You decide to leave the briefcase. Instead, caution will be the rule of the day. You know that you must be ever on the alert, and on top of all that, you must concentrate on the race.

Morning comes after a fitful night's sleep. Marie-Lise greets you with enthusiasm. "There you are, sleepyhead," she says. "Let's go look at the course on Mt. Ventoux. Come on, hurry."

Cousin Hubert, who arrived late last night, nods his head in agreement, then turns back to his cup of coffee.

Forty minutes later, you and Marie-Lise enter the first climbing turn on the road up Mt. Ventoux. You shift down into second, and the car rockets up and around the curve.

"Average speed! Remember, average speed is the important thing. You don't have to prove anything," Marie-Lise says, looking down at her clipboard. Two stopwatches hang around her neck. "Try to get to the top, about eleven miles, in twenty-one minutes. You don't need to be a speed demon. Got it?"

"Got it," you reply.

Turn to page 49.

"We should have stopped," you say, realizing the man really was in need of help.

"But we didn't. Don't feel guilty," Marie-Lise comments. "You made your decision. There was no way for you to know. Don't be too hard on yourself."

You acknowledge what she says, but guilt does linger. There is nothing you can do now, so you both continue on.

For five days you and Marie-Lise trade the driving duties over high passes, along narrow twisting roads, around an oval racetrack, and through traffic in several crowded towns. You finally finish the race back in Marseilles.

Turn to page 59.

You relax, but you are also alert. The wheel feels natural and alive in your hands. You heel-and-toe both the clutch and the brake as you have been taught by Hubert, and the Porsche heads up the sides of Mt. Ventoux with purpose and discipline.

"Good, really good," Marie-Lise remarks as you pass a roadside marker. You're pleased with her compliment, and you love the feel of the car under your control.

"Yikes!" you shout suddenly as a large black Mercedes comes rocketing down the road, hogging the middle and leaving little room for you.

Your instincts take over as you move the wheel deftly and correctly. You barely squirt by the Mercedes.

"Who was that?" you ask, out of breath.

"An idiot!" Marie-Lise exclaims as she watches the quickly departing car out of the back window. "If I didn't know better, I'd say he was out to kill us."

Her words reverberate in your head. You agree with her, they were trying to run you off the road. But why?

Turn to the next page.

50

The next section of three miles is uneventful. Marie-Lise keeps a sharp eye out for any type of hazard. She also keeps her eyes peeled for cars with the intent to do harm.

You finally approach the summit, marked by a tall radio tower. You come to a stop at the base of the tower, and you turn to Marie-Lise, checking the time and the average speed. "Well, how'd we do?"

"Not bad, not bad at all," she says proudly. "You are within three seconds of the projected arrival time. Good enough! So, how'd you like it?"

"I loved it," you reply.

Turn to page 58.

You stammer a refusal to Raoul's offer, mentioning that there are some things that you want to attend to personally on the Ferrari.

"Good for you," Raoul says. "I like a person who has their priorities right. Henri will stay with you. I'm off to meet a friend. See you later."

The rest of the day trails off in streams of work and excitement. Near three o'clock that afternoon, Hubert approaches you. "You seem upset. What's the matter?" he asks.

"Pre-race jitters, I guess," you reply.

"No, it's more than that," he persists.

Turn to the next page.

"Well, to tell you the truth, Raoul and Henri bother me. I feel it in my bones. They can't be trusted."

"You know, I agree. Something about Henri scares me. Can't put my finger on it, but—"

"I'd rather we were on our own," you press on.

"Done! It's good to follow instincts," Hubert says. "Leave it to me, I'll handle it."

Two hours later, with Henri now gone, you and Hubert sit by the big Ferrari sipping coffee and soda and munching on some sandwiches.

Go on to the next page.

"Let's talk strategy," Hubert says, finishing the last of his coffee.

"Great, I'm ready," you reply.

"You will be up against some of the old-time heroes of this sport. They mean business today as much as they did thirty years ago. Make no mistake, this is no Sunday outing."

"I understand," you say. "Continue."

"I know you know most of this, but let's go over it again. Stirling Moss, arguably the finest driver of all time, says that driving is . . ."

Before Hubert can finish, you rattle them off. "Balance, smoothness, relaxation, urgency, forcefulness, reactions, and a practical mind."

"Very good," Hubert exclaims. "Don't forget, cornering is the key to it all."

Turn to the next page.

54

"Tell me about slipstreaming, Hubert," you ask. You have heard about this many times, but you like to hear him tell it.

"Oh, an art! Moss was the greatest of the slipstreamers. He would get on Fangio's tail like a mosquito, and no matter what Fangio did, there was Moss no more than ten feet behind him. Ten feet, mind you, and at a hundred and twenty miles per hour! It would drive Fangio mad to see Moss on his tail. And Moss was getting a free ride—saving gas, pushing Fangio, and making him wear his brakes. Ah, those were the days!"

"Bike racers do that too," you comment. Back home you ride with a group of young racers. Slipstreaming is not new to you. It can be dangerous in bicycle racing. One slip and a whole pack of you can go down. In auto racing, a slip and you are sure to crash.

"This is no bike race. Remember that it is only for fun. Don't risk your life. It's not worth it," Hubert warns.

"That reminds me, what about Raoul and Henri?" you ask, worried.

"I don't know. Leave them alone, I suppose. You'll find those types at racetracks all over the world. Con men," Hubert says nonchalantly.

Turn to the next page.

56

When you return to the hotel that night, there is a letter waiting for you at the front desk. Hubert doesn't see it, and you don't tell him about it. It's probably just as well. He's got enough to worry about now.

When you open the letter, you're surprised by what you see.

> Be careful, my young friend. Be careful in the race. Death lurks on this racecourse. Keep a good distance between yourself and all other cars. Trust no one, and be on the lookout at all times. I know. I am your friend.
> Raoul

Go on to the next page.

You puzzle over the note's meaning. Is this just a friendly warning, or is there a more sinister meaning behind it? Maybe you should find Raoul and confront him with the letter. But maybe he didn't really write it. Things are certainly beginning to become complicated!

*If you choose to search out Raoul,
turn to page 94.*

*If you choose to ignore the note,
turn to page 103.*

58

The drive back to Venasque is uneventful. Marie-Lise takes the wheel. Because the rally is long, the navigator also serves as relief driver.

When you reach the hotel, Hubert greets you outside. "Time to push on, my friends. Let's get the tires in Avignon and then head on to Marseilles. By the way, that fellow Raoul, he left right after you two. He said to tell you that curiosity can kill the cat. What's going on?"

"What do you know of Raoul?" you ask Marie-Lise.

"He's a friend of my uncle's. My father says he's shifty. He's always been nice to me, but I don't really trust him."

"We'll be careful," you say, but you have a nagging feeling that Raoul is up to no good. You want to tell Hubert about your psychic Paris experience. But it is a bit of an embarrassment. You don't know if Hubert would believe you. You don't even wholly believe it yourself. It was just a dream, or was it?

If you decide to say nothing, turn to page 65.

If you decide to tell Hubert about the conversation in Paris, turn to page 84.

You are not the winner of your class—far from it, in fact. But you admirably competed and finished the circuit, and you should be proud.

Raoul and the others never even showed their faces. Perhaps they stumbled across a richer game, or they got scared off. You will probably never know. And for now, it's just as well.

The End

Within half an hour you come across pictures of Eric and Raoul. "These two, they are the ones!" you exclaim.

"Perfect!" Bernard cries. "These two are con artists. They specialize in gambling and extortion. They're also kidnappers and murderers."

"I can't believe it," Marie-Lise says, shocked by this turn of events.

"Well, why don't you arrest them?" you ask, anxious for these people to be brought to justice.

"Not so easy, my young friend. We need evidence. But you could be our bait. Obviously they are on your track already."

"Why me?" you ask.

Go on to the next page.

"Your cousin Hubert tells me that you come from an enormously wealthy family. They may be planning to kidnap you. Who knows?" Bernard turns to his two companions and speaks to them in rapid Parisian French that is almost too fast for you to understand. Then he turns back to you.

"It is agreed. We will place an undercover agent in the rally. This agent will keep an eye on things. We will not tell you who he or she is—it's best if you don't know. We will be here in Venasque with the helicopter, monitoring the whole thing. You will use this miniature recording device in the event that Raoul or his henchmen approach you. Agreed?"

You hardly have time to think, but you agree immediately. "Okay. I'll do it. But shouldn't I be armed?" you ask.

"No. That only encourages trouble. We will put one electronic homing device on your car and one on your shirt. They will be more helpful than any gun." Bernard signals to one of his aides, who attaches a harmless-looking pin to your shirt. He places another in the back of the Porsche.

Turn to the next page.

62

"Remember, we will be monitoring you the whole way. Have courage, be careful, and good luck."

"Let's go," Hubert says. He is somewhat grim-faced. "I don't like putting you in this situation. Maybe you'd prefer to withdraw and return to the States."

"No, I'm in it all the way," you reply.

Go on to the next page.

Hubert nods his agreement and his approval. You and Marie-Lise leave in the Porsche, followed by Hubert in the Range Rover. The stop for the tires in Avignon is brief, and later that day you are in Marseilles, at the site of the Alpine Rally.

Before you know it, it is the morning of the race. You are awake and up before dawn, checking the maps and going over the stages of the rally. You are ready to go, and so far there has been no trouble with Raoul and his companions.

The officials note your car number and give you the start sign.

You're off! The first stage involves getting to the top of Mt. Ventoux in three hours and six minutes. Getting out of Marseilles is a job in and of itself. It is a large and bustling city, but you make it with only minor difficulty.

Turn to the next page.

64

"Warn me before the exit. What is the town?" you ask Marie-Lise.

"Carpentras," she replies. "It's about fifty miles from here. I'll give you plenty of warning."

The time goes by quickly, and soon you are heading off the expressway and onto the back roads from Carpentras to Mt. Ventoux. The roads are narrow and full of sharp turns and squiggles.

"Increase your speed about ten miles per hour," Marie-Lise tells you.

"No problem," you respond, keeping an eye on the tachometer as well as on the speedometer.

Turn to page 70.

Your decision to say nothing of your café experience begins a fateful turn of events.

Raoul and his right-hand man, Henri, have been keeping an eye on you and Hubert. This is what they are up to:

"The coast is clear, my friend," Raoul says to Henri. "Hubert will be kept busy, and we will have a nice little business deal on our hands."

"You talk big, but let's wait and see," Henri replies.

"Your skepticism keeps me on my toes, Henri," Raoul says, his eyes shining. "We will intercept the American in Marseilles. Leave it to me."

"As you wish, Raoul, as you wish," Henri replies.

The two of them leave Venasque and head straight for Marseilles.

That evening, Raoul and his gang make their final plans.

"It's very simple," he says. "We approach the American with a plan that is so good that refusal will be impossible. The rally is compromised, money changes hands, and presto—either the family pays us to shut up, or we turn the evidence over to the police. We, of course, remain anonymous. Perfect, no?"

Turn to the next page.

"Too complicated, Raoul," Eric says, frowning. "It's much easier to grab the American on course. Rally driver disappears, family distraught, no evidence of foul play, etc."

"Let's have a vote," the auburn-haired woman suggests. Henri scowls.

"Okay, all in favor of blackmail say 'Oui'; opposed, 'Non.'"

The vote is quick.

"The 'nons' have it," Eric announces. "So, kidnapping it is. Good, I'm greatly relieved. Blackmail seldom works well."

"Have it your way. I withdraw," Raoul says and stalks out of the room.

"Just as well," Henri comments. "I've never liked the man. He's too dishonest."

"Coming from you, Henri, it is a compliment," Eric says laughing.

Turn to page 69.

You've come too far to let these hoodlums stop you now, you decide. "Step aside!" you shout as you accelerate the Porsche and sideswipe the car in front of you.

The car moves just enough for you to squeak by, and you manage to get up some speed. But the next hairpin comes up too quickly. Even though there is only a two-hundred-foot drop at this point, it is enough to end your racing career forever.

The End

Meanwhile, you and Marie-Lise start the Alpine Rally, oblivious to the plans of Eric and his gang. You worry about them, but the rally takes control of your attention.

The first leg up Mt. Ventoux is marked by a heart attack for one of the competitors. Aside from that, all goes fairly well. The next day is more difficult. A tire blows on the gravel road of a mountain pass in Italy. It takes more time than you thought to change the tire, and suddenly you and Marie-Lise are six minutes behind on that stage of the course.

"We'll never make it up," she comments.

"Yes we will," you reply as you race the Porsche up the hairpin turns of the mountain road. Fortunately there are no other cars nearby. Suddenly, before you have time to think, a blood-red Zagato Alpha passes you on a curve, coming dangerously close. You haven't the faintest idea where it came from!

"That was close," you comment.

"We made it, that's what counts," Marie-Lise says, relieved.

Turn to page 75.

Moments later you are on the familiar road up the mountain. Two Zagato Alphas zoom past you, followed moments later by a green Healy 3000. You know that they are competitors by the numbers on their hoods.

"Slow down," Marie-Lise says, "we're ahead of schedule by about two minutes."

Up ahead, a small tan Sunbeam Talbot with numbers on the hood comes into view. It's stretched across the road, almost completely blocking it. A man stands by its side waving a white cloth like a flag.

There is something about the man that doesn't seem right—this could be a trap. Then again, maybe he really needs help.

If you decide to stop, turn to page 79.

If you decide to ignore the man and continue on, turn to page 83.

Slowly you open the car door and step out dejectedly onto the road. You have one more trick up your sleeve. You decide to wait and see what happens. "What do you want?"

"You, that's all. As for you, Marie-Lise, you'd be smart to keep quiet. If you don't, then your poor papa will pay a dreadful price. We know about some of his financial dealings in Latin America."

"You can't do this, Uncle Eric!" Marie-Lise screams.

"Wrong, we are doing it. You will report that this American left the rally. You will finish. Understand? Remember, your father's reputation is at stake. Be smart and listen to me."

"Take this, you rat," you shout, spraying a can of starting fluid into Eric's face.

Before anyone can react, you grab Marie-Lise's hand and are over the side of the road, tumbling down the slope of the hill. You slide over rocks, bushes, and piles of gravel and make it to the next run in the road just as a string of cars comes by.

Turn to the next page.

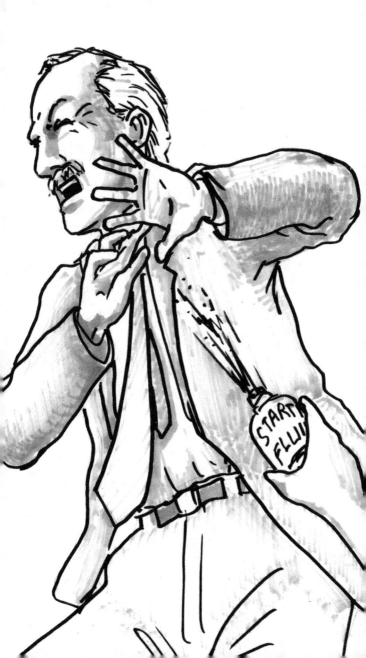

"Help!" you shout.

The third car in the string skids to a halt, and both you and Marie-Lise pile aboard. "Police!" you exclaim.

The driver doesn't wait for an explanation. He nods, then accelerates down the twisting road.

"Darndest rally I've ever been in," the navigator says calmly, turning his attention to his maps and watches. "Police at the next checkpoint, I think."

The first rally of your career may be over, but now that you are safe, the future is sure to bring great successes in rally driving.

The End

"Keep on pushing," Marie-Lise says. "We're making up time."

"Right," you mumble. But the strain of driving is beginning to get to you.

Three more curves and you reach a straight stretch. You push down on the accelerator, and the Porsche hungrily eats up the miles.

As you round another curve, you slam on your brakes. Three people and a car block the road.

"What's this all about?" you yell out the window.

"Get out," Eric says. "Marie-Lise, do as I say, quickly."

You are caught off guard, but a sudden flood of courage surges through you. You look at Marie-Lise, wondering whether you should get out of the car as they ask, or if you should try and escape. Whatever your decision, you have to make it now.

If you stay in the car and try to escape, turn to page 67.

If you get out of the car, turn to page 72.

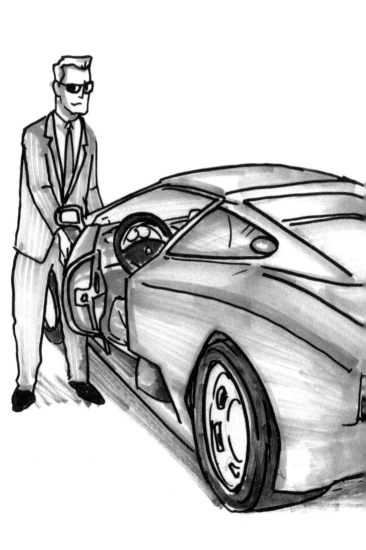

"I can't refuse an offer like that, Raoul. Let's go," you say, carried away by the moment.

"I knew you'd come. We're alike, you and I. I could see that right off," he says, laughing.

Raoul opens the driver's door, and you slip behind the wheel of this space-age machine. The dials and gauges confronting you look like a control panel from a supersonic fighter.

You slip the key into the groove. A turn and the engine bursts into a hearty roar. The lights on the dash blink, giving you some information you need, and a lot that you don't.

"Let's go. Turn right at the end of the driveway," Raoul says as he leans back in his seat, selects a CD from the glove compartment, and inserts it into the player. The sound of jazz fills the inside of the car, and you almost feel as if you are inside the music.

Turn to the next page.

78

Letting out the clutch slowly, you feel the car move with precision. The road to the right of the driveway is narrow but well surfaced.

Second gear, feed in the gas.

Third gear, your eyes flick to the tachometer, checking the revs.

Fourth gear, the car is alive and speeding along the road, eating up the turns easily. You feel free and powerful as the music pounds in your ears and runs through your body.

"Take the next left," Raoul commands pleasantly.

You obey. Ahead of you is the entrance to the Nürburgring.

Turn to page 86.

"I can't just let this guy stand there. We have time to spare, don't we?" you ask, applying the brakes.

"Yes, we do. Not too much though. A minute or two, no more."

"Okay, I'll be quick," you say, bringing the car to a halt.

"What's up?" you ask out the window.

"Thanks for stopping," the man says in an English accent. "My navigator seems to be having a problem." He indicates a slumped figure in the front of the car. "I think he's having a heart attack!"

You took a first aid course back in the States. You immediately jump out and race to the car.

"How long has he been this way?" you ask.

"Started about an hour ago, but we just pulled over."

"There's no time to waste, he might be in cardiac arrest. Get him out, quick," you order.

Turn to the next page.

The man lies on the side of the road, and you begin the proper cardiac pulmonary resuscitation procedure. It's hard work, but within three minutes you feel an erratic pulse. A staccato breathing begins, and the man rolls his eyes. His face is pale, and his skin is clammy to the touch.

"Get an ambulance!" you shout to Marie-Lise.

Go on to the next page.

Marie-Lise scrambles into the driver's seat of the Porsche and accelerates up the road in a cloud of dirt and sand.

Before long an ambulance arrives, and the semiconscious man is bundled up and driven away. A race official, complete with clipboard, stopwatches, and chronometers approaches you.

"You responsible for saving that man's life?" he asks. His accent is German, but his English is perfect.

"Yes, I guess so."

"We're willing to discount the time you lost on this section of the rally. You may continue without penalty. We wish you the best of luck. Well done," he says, extending his hand and shaking yours.

A carload of reporters and photographers who are following the rally are busily snapping photos and talking to the driver of the Sunbeam Talbot. They are moving toward you, but you duck the photo session.

Turn to the next page.

82

Later that night, as you and Marie-Lise cross into Italy, you reflect on the day. You can't help but wonder what happened to Raoul and the others. If they escape, you will never feel free. After this race, you decide you will go back to Interpol and work with them until these criminals are all behind bars. It'll mean the end of auto racing for you this summer, but somehow you are not too disappointed.

The End

"No time to stop," you say as you pass the car. "It's probably a trick anyway—Raoul and his buddies. What do you think?"

"I'm not sure what to think," Marie-Lise replies. "All that business about Raoul is most upsetting. Uncle Eric has always been the black sheep of the family, but this—!"

You round the final turns of the steep section of the road with ease. Marie-Lise counts off the seconds as you approach the checkpoint at the top of the mountain. "Slow down, there it is!" she shouts.

Three men with clipboards stand by a small folding table. They peer at your number, and one notes it on his sheet.

"Two seconds early. Well done—no penalty," one man announces. "Carry on."

You pop the clutch, and the Porsche speeds down the mountain the way you have just come. The next checkpoint is in Italy, over the French border. It is a long and difficult haul. Despite fatigue, the two of you are going to have to be on your toes.

When you pass the Sunbeam Talbot again, the driver is leaning over the inert body of a man on the side of the road. Three other cars have stopped, and several people are kneeling down next to him. One man seems to be giving CPR.

Turn to page 47.

84

Your decision to tell Hubert about your café experience turns out to be a good one. Hubert and Marie-Lise listen with rapt attention. When you finish, Hubert says, "It's not important to question why or how this journey occurred. What is important is that we act. We will call the head of Interpol, the international police force, and hope they'll believe us."

Five hours later an Alouette helicopter sets down on the soccer field outside the town. Three men in well-cut suits get out. One of them introduces himself.

"I am Bernard Rossignol, head of the gambling division. Perhaps you can help us by looking at this book of photos." He hands over a thick, three-hinged binder.

Turn to page 60.

You enter the start-and-finish loop. It is a well-designed track. For just a moment you imagine the great races of the past. You can hear the engines, the changing of the gears, and the squeal of the tires as the glorious machines of yesteryear speed through corners. You can smell the fuel and hear the roar of the crowd in the stands.

Almost too suddenly you shift back to the present. "What now, Raoul?" you ask.

"I want you to meet a friend of mine. Her name is Celeste. She's a columnist for *The Sporting*

News and she's here to cover this race. You will like her."

"Great. Where do we find her?"

"Over by the pits. See that one?" Raoul points to an empty pit area. Many of the others are occupied by Mercedes, Alphas, Ferraris, and Gordinis.

You pull over to the area indicated. A tall woman with auburn hair dressed in a white jumpsuit waves and smiles at you.

Turn to the next page.

"That's Celeste," Raoul comments. He pushes a button, and the music stops. It's almost a relief not to be surrounded by sound any longer.

Celeste runs over. "You must be the American driver we have heard so much about," she says.

You wonder how she has heard about you, and there is a tug at your memory. Her voice is familiar, but you just can't remember where you have heard it before.

Go on to the next page.

For two hours, the three of you drive the beautiful curving circuit. The forests are enchanting, the ravines and rivers lovely. The famous Karussel turn is dangerous-looking.

Celeste seems to have an endless supply of CDs that she carries around in her handbag. She continually gives them to Raoul, who feeds them into the player. At first you are about to object, but after a while you begin to love the soothing music. The loud jazz of the first CD Raoul played is gone. Now the more soothing sounds of a German fusion group fill the car. You like it. There is something almost hypnotic about it.

At last you pull to a stop by a restaurant.

'Time for lunch," Raoul announces.

You are famished. It's been a long and exhausting day. You welcome the break.

There are only a few people at the restaurant, and the service is quick and competent. Soon the three of you are all alone, except for the waiter who has retired to a corner to read a newspaper.

Turn to the next page.

90

Raoul stares at you, his eyes powerful and almost fierce. There is a light in them that transfixes you. "Our dear, new friend, we have a proposal for you," he says. "It is one that you cannot refuse."

"Raoul is right," Celeste adds. Her voice is modulated and smooth.

Go on to the next page.

"Well, what is it?" you ask, a shiver of apprehension running up your spine.

Before they answer, Celeste removes a small portable CD player, inserts a disc, and turns it on. You immediately recognize it as the one that Raoul played when you first drove the car. It seems to overtake you, and you suddenly feel as though you are spinning out of control.

"Would you please turn that off," you say.

"In a moment," Celeste snaps.

Go on to the next page.

92

"What we want you to do is drive the race as well as you can," Raoul says.

"Of course," you reply, somewhat confused by this statement. Do they think that you wouldn't?

"Yes, of course. But if we give you a signal, a simple signal like holding up a purple card about the size of a magazine, we want you to slow down, just enough to lose the race. If we hold up the purple card. Understand? You will be well rewarded. Make no mistake about that," Raoul explains.

"But, why?" you ask, stalling for time. The music seems to be winding its way into your brain and your ability to reason. You fight it, making a conscious effort to override it. Reaching out, you click off the CD player.

Go on to the next page.

"Don't be difficult," Celeste says impatiently. "Listen to Raoul."

Your brain and will are engaged in a battle. It seems as though your brain is still responding to the hidden messages in the music. But your will comes back strong, little by little.

How to get out of this mess is the question. Resisting these people could be dangerous—they may be armed. Perhaps you should play along with them for a while. On the other hand, if you distract them somehow, you might just make a break for it.

*If you decide to make a break for it,
turn to page 96.*

If you decide to play along, turn to page 106.

94

After dinner, you excuse yourself and go out for a walk. Once outside, you make for the Range Rover and take a quick trip to Raoul's hotel. Raoul's note was written on hotel stationery; you assume that he will be there.

Your assumption is correct, but the welcome you get is not what you expected. Along with Raoul and Henri, an auburn-haired woman, a dark-haired man, and a white-haired man greet you less than kindly. You recognize them all from the café in Paris.

"We don't like being ignored," Raoul says, starting toward you. The white-haired man stops him, placing a hand on his forearm.

"What Raoul means, my fine American friend, is that you seem to be making the wrong decisions. You don't know us, but we know all about you."

"Maybe," you reply, edging toward the door. Henri steps in front of you.

"No maybes about it," the white-haired man continues. "We want your cooperation, or you will not survive the race. We are prepared to be generous, and we are not greedy or evil. Just business-oriented, that's all. That should be easy for an American to understand. This race is a business opportunity. Join us or the consequences will be less than pleasant."

Go on to the next page.

"I don't think so," you reply, reaching down inside yourself for all the calmness and courage that you can muster. "I took the trouble to call Interpol before I came here. If I'm not mistaken, they are in the business of interrupting games like yours."

The door swings open, and three men holding automatic weapons enter the room.

"Please place your hands on the wall. We have recorded this conversation, and may I add, we have been looking for you, Mr. Raoul des Jardins, since the incident in Monte Carlo." The speaker is the head of the gambling division of Interpol.

Raoul and Henri, along with the others, are led away.

Six days later you compete in the Nürburgring and place a respectable fourth in your class. You may not have won, but you did get to finish. And after all you've been through, you feel more than proud.

The End

96

"You're playing with fire," you say as calmly as possible, waiting for an opportunity to make a break for it.

"Button your lip," Celeste snaps at you.

"Oh, yeah?" Instantly you jump up and pull on the tablecloth so that the hot bowls of thick goulash spill all over Raoul and Celeste.

"You're in for it now," Raoul shouts, jumping back from the table.

"Idiot!" Celeste shrieks.

You are off! And not a minute to spare.

The Maserati stands ready for action, but you think better of it, and run for the woods.

Turn to the next page.

You come to rest about a hundred yards into the forest, your breath coming short and fast. Enormous oaks, beeches, pines, and hemlocks tower around you, but there is little undergrowth. Hiding will not be too easy.

It takes several minutes for your heart to slow its furious beating. Refreshed, you head deeper into the forest.

"Which way?" you hear Raoul shout.

"I don't know!" Celeste answers angrily.

"You go north, I'll circle back. We'll catch that brat!"

You move as quietly as possible, keeping out of sight. Soon you are back at the restaurant, but there in the entranceway stand Eric and the short young man from the café in Paris. They are busy questioning the waiter, so they don't see you.

"We will wait here, Eric," the younger man says. "There is no sense in chasing off into the woods. The American couldn't have gone far."

"Watch the cars," Eric cautions.

"Don't worry, no one will get by me," the other man says with an air of menace.

Go on to the next page.

Then you hear the unmistakable noise of a pack of kids marching along on a camping trip. They are shouting and singing, fighting and bickering. Over this discord comes the voice of an older male, the counselor, you imagine. He shouts orders and commands, but no one obeys.

The group finally breaks into view. It's a pack of about thirty boys and girls.

This unruly bunch doesn't walk in any form of order, and some of the kids are your size, so it is easy for you to join in at the tail end without being noticed. The counselor is a red-haired young man. You move up to him, greeting him in your school German.

"Hello, how are you," you say.

"Fine, thanks," he replies.

"I'm an American," you continue as you pass the restaurant and walk up a path on the far side of the parking lot.

"So, what's your name?" he asks.

You tell him.

"My name is Karl," he says, and the two of you shake hands.

Turn to the next page.

100

You continue your conversation with Karl until finally you reach a large old Mercedes bus.

"Would you like to come with us?" Karl asks you.

"I sure would," you reply, swinging aboard the bus. Karl fires up the old engine, and with a burst of exhaust, you leave the forest restaurant behind and head for the town of Nürburg. You'll find a police station there, for sure; however, you worry that without any proof to your fantastic story, no one will believe you.

"Karl, will you let me off in the center of town?" you ask.

"Of course. But then come have dinner with us later tonight," he says.

"It will be my pleasure," you reply. "I've got a few things to take care of first."

Turn to the next page.

102

Moments later you're telling your story to the police commander, but you leave out the part about the café in Paris. After all, you can't really be sure that actually happened.

Later that night, you celebrate your adventure with Karl and his group of young rascals. Hubert joins you, upset at what you have been through. But you console him.

"Don't worry, Hubert, I enjoyed it," you tell him. "This has been the most exciting summer ever!"

P.S. You win the race!!

The End

Some things are not worth bothering with, you decide. You crumple up Raoul's note and toss it in the wastebasket of your room. From now on it's pure concentration on the race. You dismiss your feelings about the five people in the Trois Copains.

In the mornings, you drive the course in the Range Rover, and in the afternoons, you work on the Ferrari, taking it out for spins on the start/finish loop. The car handles beautifully despite its enormous power and tall gearing.

The tension builds as crowds of racing fans swarm into town. Fields become multicolored campgrounds overnight. The red, blue, green, yellow, and orange tents look like wildflowers from a distance. Exotic sports cars ranging from Mercedes chain drives to Talbot Lagos and Hispano-Suizas putter about the now-crowded roads around Nürburg.

You return to find Hubert trembling, his head in his hands.

"Hubert, what happened?"

"That was the closest ever, I should be dead. I just missed two cars that collided and caught fire. Horrible. It's all foolishness, really."

"What, what's foolish," you ask not sure what foolishness he's referring to.

"This, all this."

"The world goes hungry, and we spend all of our time and money on these toys. I think I've just woken up!"

Turn to page 109.

Sure enough, about six kilometers down the road you enter the town of Nürburg, and next to the Rathaus—the town hall—is the police station. But the reception you get is far from what you expected. They begin by arresting you for stealing a car and running out on your restaurant bill. Your explanations are greeted with amused disbelief. You are in for a long afternoon, and Raoul and the gang are sure to make their escape.

While you are being interrogated, Raoul arrives, coolly takes possession of his Maserati, and disappears.

"Now my young friend, why did you steal the car?" the police commander asks. "We have a complaint right here!" He waves a document at you.

"But, I didn't . . ." you reply. The chief smiles, but it is not a friendly smile. Time marches slowly by, and you wish with all your might that your cousin would show up. You know you can explain things to Hubert. But how you're going to convince the police is another matter.

The End

106

"Okay. What's my share?" you say.

Raoul smiles and takes a sip of his coffee. "You learn fast, don't you? Well, I'm not surprised. America is ruled by money. Your split? Well let's say that we'll give you enough to keep you in new sports cars for more than a lifetime."

"All I have to do is throw the race, is that it?" you ask.

"If we see fit to have you do that, yes. Maybe it won't happen that way."

"How will you control the other cars?" you ask.

"We have our ways. Don't worry about that," Celeste chimes in.

"You were all in the Trois Copains café in Paris together, weren't you?" you suddenly blurt out. The memory of that event in Paris rushes back to you. But wait a minute. Wasn't it all a dream?

"The rat knows! We've been set up," Celeste shrieks. Fear and surprise flush her face.

"Be calm. I'll handle this," Raoul says. "How much do you want?" he asks, eyes flashing.

"More than you will ever be able to offer me," you reply.

Raoul's face also turns red. "Greedy, aren't you?" he says.

Go on to the next page.

Your mind speeds ahead, formulating a plan. It's risky, but it's all that you can do for the moment.

"I am not alone. Hubert is a member of Interpol," you say as calmly as you can. "At this very minute he is monitoring our meeting. If you don't believe me, then ask your friend Eric."

"How do you know about him?" Raoul says, his control ebbing quickly. Fear is visible on his handsome face.

"He's an informer. The other two fellows from the café are under our control as well. So, what will it be? Will you go with me quietly, or shall I be forced to signal for the police?" You hope your bluff works.

"You're making this up," Celeste replies, beginning to regain her composure.

"No, I'm not. You want more proof? Okay, then. Henri, your mechanic, drove a moped to the café. Right?"

Raoul and Celeste eye each other, amazed and frightened.

"Don't deny it. Give up and come quietly." You signal for the waiter. He moves briskly to your side.

"Be sure these people don't leave without paying the check. I'm going to make a telephone call," you say calmly.

Turn to the next page.

108

You get up and run. Raoul and Celeste are so surprised that they don't make a move for several seconds. It is just enough time for you to get to the Maserati. The keys are still in the ignition.

"Start, you devil! Start!" you command the car. It does just that, and with the clutch popped, you zoom off.

The car behaves as if it were a part of your own body. It seems to anticipate turns and the approach of other cars on the narrow roads.

"Police, that's what I need," you say out loud. "Nürburg, I'll bet there's a station there."

Turn to page 105.

You are shocked by Hubert's sudden change in attitude.

"But, Hubert, you love all this. What's wrong?" you say, bewildered by his words.

"It comes to me at times like this. My work in the bank just deals with money. It's all people seem to want. The people I see, anyway. But when I go to Africa to check out a factory we are helping to finance, or when I'm in India, it's a different story. People starve—whole families—while we play with these expensive toys. It doesn't make sense, does it?" He looks at you, and you suddenly hear what he is saying.

"Let's do something about it," you say, always ready for a change.

"But what?" Hubert says, sounding hopeless.

"Let's quit the race. Sell the car. Let's spend our time working on some UN project. You know those guys in the UN in Geneva. Let's go to them. I've got almost a whole summer left."

Hubert regards you with interest. "You're willing to give this up? This race, this world of excitement?"

"Why not, Hubert? After all, does it really matter whether one car beats another? Does it really matter?" you ask, surprising yourself.

Turn to the next page.

"You sound so much older than your years, cousin. We can't do much in the summer you have remaining, but we can make a start. For years I've felt bad about spending all this time and money on these cars. I just didn't want to disappoint you this summer."

"Hubert, you're not only my cousin, you're my friend and guide," you say.

"No, you are a guide, too. Your willingness to turn from racing to an uncertain and difficult task makes me feel all the stronger. Thank you, cousin."

"Let's get going," you say. Images of the Sahel region in Africa fill your mind—this is where the Sahara desert is expanding each year and driving the farmers and herders away from their home-land. Starvation stalks them wherever they go. "Let's see the UN people right away. Maybe we could get involved in some kind of technical project with water wells. You know, drilling them, irrigating the fields."

"It's a starting point. But shall we stay another day and watch the race?" Hubert says with just a tinge of nostalgic regret in his voice.

"No, it's time to leave," you say, as feelings of regret and sadness mingle inside you, too. But you've make up your mind, there's no going back. You know that new and exciting adventures await you.

The End

ABOUT THE ARTISTS

Illustrator: Wes Louie was born and raised in Los Angeles, where he grew up drawing. He attended Pasadena City College, where he made a lot of great friends and contacts, and then the Art Center. Wes majored in illustration, but also took classes in industrial design and entertainment. He has been working in the entertainment industry

Illustrator: Sittisan Sundaravej (Quan). Sittisan is a resident of Bangkok, Thailand and an old fan of *Choose Your Own Adventure*. He attended The University of the Arts in Philadelphia, where he received his BSC in Architecture and a BFA in Animation. He has been a 2D and 3D animation director for productions in Asia and the United States and is a freelance illustrator.

ABOUT THE AUTHOR

R. A. MONTGOMERY has hiked in the Hima-
layas, climbed mountains in Europe, scuba-dived in
Central America, and worked in Africa. He lives in
France in the winter, travels frequently to Asia, and
calls Vermont home. Montgomery graduated from
Williams College and attended graduate school at
Yale University and NYU. His interests include
macroeconomics, geopolitics, mythology, history,
mystery novels, and music. He has two grown sons,
a daughter-in-law, and two granddaughters. His
wife, Shannon Gilligan, is an author and noted
interactive game designer. Montgomery feels that
the generation of people under 15 is the most
important asset in our world.

**Visit us online at www.cyoa.com for games
and other fun stuff, or to write to
R. A. Montgomery!**

ADVENTURER'S LOG

ADVENTURER'S LOG

ADVENTURER'S LOG

ADVENTURER'S LOG

ADVENTURER'S LOG

ADVENTURER'S LOG

ADVENTURER'S LOG

ADVENTURER'S LOG

ADVENTURER'S LOG

ADVENTURER'S LOG

ADVENTURER'S LOG

ADVENTURER'S LOG

ADVENTURER'S LOG

ADVENTURER'S LOG

ADVENTURER'S LOG

ADVENTURER'S LOG

ADVENTURER'S LOG

ADVENTURER'S LOG

ADVENTURER'S LOG

ADVENTURER'S LOG

ADVENTURER'S LOG

ADVENTURER'S LOG